To Mom and Dad

Visit us on the Web! www.randomhouse.com/kids

Educators and librarians, for a variety of teaching tools,
visit us at www.randomhouse.com/teachers

Visit Penny at www.myprettypenny.com

Library of Congress Cataloging-in-Publication Data
Kinch, Devon.
Pretty Penny sets up shop / Devon Kinch. — 1st ed.
p. cm.
Summary: Six-year-old Pretty Penny wants to have a birthday party for her
grandmother, but first she must earn some money.
ISBN 978-0-375-86735-4 (trade) — ISBN 978-0-375-96737-5 (lib. bdg.)
[1. Moneymaking projects—Fiction. 2. Grandmothers—Fiction.] I. Title.
PZ7.K5653Pr 2011
[E]—dc22
2010003441

MANUFACTURED IN CHINA
10 9 8 7 6 5 4 3 2 1
First Edition

Pretty Penny

SETS
UP
SHOP

DEVON KINCH

RANDOM HOUSE 🏠 NEW YORK

This is Pretty Penny, but you can call her Penny. Her two favorite colors are pink and black, and she has a pet pig named Iggy.

Lots of people tell her she has very big ideas for a girl so small.

Like the time she wrote her first novel. That was a
really big idea. Or the time she held a puppy-dog fashion
show. Now, that was a really, really big idea!

PENNY'S →SPRING← COLLECTION!

Every summer Penny stays with her grandma Bunny.
She is an artist. Her cat, Bo, models for her sometimes.

Bunny owns this yellow building from top to bottom.
She lives on the parlor floor and rents out three tidy
apartments to neighbors. The tippy-top floor is the attic.
It is where Bunny keeps all of her extra stuff.

And she has a lot of extra stuff.

Saturday is Bunny's birthday. This year Bunny does not want a party.

"There is no reason to spend money on a party for a little ol' lady like me," Bunny insists.

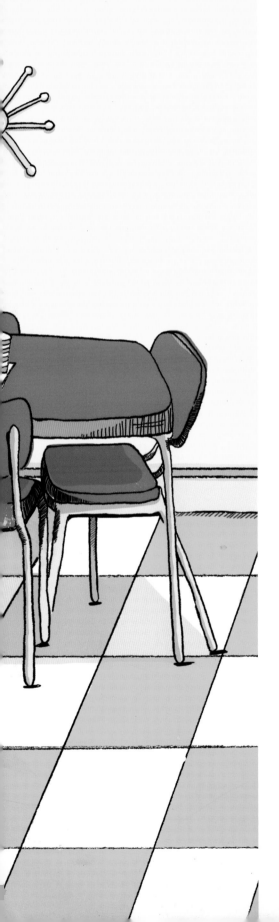

Penny is upset. She must
find a way to have a birthday
party for Bunny without
spending too much money.

Wait, she doesn't have
any money! Where will she
get it? How will she earn it?

She racks her brain for one of her big ideas. Nothing comes to her.

She just has to wait.
And wait some more . . .

Suddenly she has it—
a really big idea!

She runs to the attic door
and takes a peek up the stairs.

The attic is full of treasures!

Penny finds a fancy dress, a cozy scarf, a silly hat, an adorable old teddy bear, a cuckoo clock, loads of interesting books, and even an antique telephone!

"All right, Penny, what's going on?" asks Bunny.

Bunny knows Penny is up to something. It is easy to tell because her finger points straight in the air when she has one of her big ideas.

"Can I turn the attic into a shopping mall?" asks Penny.
"That's a great idea! I would love to get rid of all this
stuff!" says Bunny. "Let's call it the Small Mall!"
It's a plan. Bunny and Penny shake hands.

Penny has a lot of work to do
to get the Small Mall ready.

She bends and lifts.

She cleans and sorts.

She zips back and forth
and up and down.

Iggy barely lifts a finger.

Then Penny makes price tags. Everything must have a price. Some things are old, some things are like new, and for some things she just has no clue.

These shoes are like new.
The price is $3.00.

This clock works perfectly.
The price is $2.00.

Batons are so much fun
and not that expensive.
The price is $1.00.

This teddy bear is missing an eye!
The price should only be 50¢.

This hat belonged to Bunny
when she was a little girl. It
must be worth a lot of money.
The price is $5.00.

Penny loves Bunny's old
dollhouse way too much
to sell it. **Not for sale!**

Penny hangs the Small Mall signs. There is one for the front
door and two for the hallway.

Every item has a price tag. Penny even has a cash register.
When the drawer opens, it makes the sound *ka-ching!*

At last, she is ready.

"Come one, come all, to the grand opening of the Small Mall!"

The Small Mall is officially open. Here come the customers! Mrs. Wilson from the second floor stops by with her daughters, Emma and Maggie. Bunny helps Mrs. Wilson pick out a pair of shoes while Iggy models earrings for the girls.

"These shoes are a real bargain. I'll take them!"
says Mrs. Wilson.

"That will be three dollars, please," says Penny.

Buck stops by to check out the toys. He lives on the third floor with his mom and dad.

"How much for this toy truck and bouncy ball?" asks Buck.

"All together, that will be two dollars and fifty cents," says Penny. "Thank you, and please come again, sir!"

"I just love this hat!" exclaims Emma.

"It looks great," says Penny. "Don't forget your receipt."

What a busy day! It is time to close the store. *Ka-ching!*
Penny takes the money out of the cash register and counts it.
She made ten dollars.

When Penny puts the money in her pink purse, Iggy raises an eyebrow. "You're right, Iggy! This is not my money—it belongs to Bunny," says Penny. She runs to the living room.

"Bunny, Bunny, Bunny, we have all your money!
Thank you for letting me sell your treasures!" says Penny.

"You can keep the money, Penny. You earned it,"
Bunny says.

Penny knows just what she'll do with the money.

On Saturday morning, Penny goes to Mr. Wilson's bakery. Cupcakes are $1.00 each.

"I'll take ten!"

Penny hurries back to Bunny's house.

She knocks on each and every neighbor's apartment door and invites them over for a surprise.

Penny tells everyone to shush.
Shush! It's very, very quiet.

"Happy birthday, Bunny!"
"A party for me?" Bunny asks
with a smile. "Now, whose big
idea was this?"